W9-BSY-989

The
BENCH

By

Meghan, The Duchess of Sussex

Pictures by Christian Robinson

Random House 🏠 New York

Copyright © 2021 by Peca Publishing, LLC

All rights reserved. Published in the United States by Random House Children's Books, a division of Penguin Random House LLC, New York.

Random House and the colophon are registered trademarks of Penguin Random House LLC.

Visit us on the Web!
rhcbooks.com

Educators and librarians, for a variety of teaching tools, visit us at RHTeachersLibrarians.com

Library of Congress Cataloging-in-Publication Data is available upon request.
ISBN 978-0-593-43451-2 (trade) — ISBN 978-0-593-43453-6 (ebook)

The artist used acrylic paint, colored pencil, and a bit of digital manipulation to create the illustrations for this book.
The text of this book is set in 17-point Jazmin. Interior design by Martha Rago and Christian Robinson.

Printed in the United States of America
10 9 8 7 6 5 4 3 2 1
First Edition

Random House Children's Books supports the First Amendment and celebrates the right to read.

Penguin Random House LLC supports copyright. Copyright fuels creativity, encourages diverse voices, promotes free speech, and creates a vibrant culture. Thank you for buying an authorized edition of this book and for complying with copyright laws by not reproducing, scanning, or distributing any part in any form without permission. You are supporting writers and allowing Penguin Random House to publish books for every reader.

For the man and the boy
who make my heart go
pump-pump

This is your bench
Where life will begin
For you and our son
Our baby, our kin.

This is your bench
Where you'll witness great joy.

From here you will rest
See the growth of our boy.

He'll learn to ride a bike
As you watch on with pride.

He'll run and he'll fall
And he'll take it in stride.

You'll love him.
You'll listen.
You'll be his supporter.

When life feels in shambles

You'll help him find order.

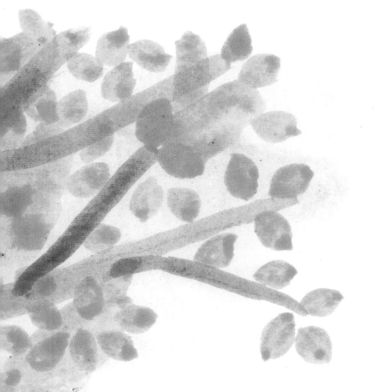

You'll sit on this bench
As his giving tree.

Some days he may cry
Perched there on your knee.

He'll feel happiness, sorrow
One day be heartbroken.

You'll tell him "I love you"
Those words always spoken.

This is your bench
For papa and son . . .

To celebrate joys
And victories won.

And here in the window
I'll have tears of great joy . . .

Looking out at My Love
And our beautiful boy.

Right there on your bench
The place you'll call home . . .

With daddy and son . . .

Where you'll never be 'lone.

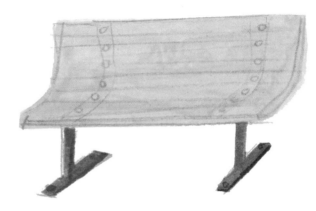

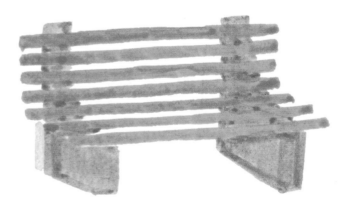